Bullet J

The Country & Western Cowboy Series

Book 2

Michael Haden

Other Books By Michael Haden

CHAPTER ONE

Sal Williams looked up from his cold beans and scratched his two-day old beard. He hated beans but beans were all he had.

The cowpoke was heading towards his home in the town of Oak Ridge. A town that still held some sentiment to him, even though he'd been away from home for so long. It is a plight similar to destiny for a man to want to return home. Nonetheless, Sal sat in the middle of his makeshift camp on the Tumbleweed Trail and wondered if the town had changed.

The Tumbleweed Trail was an old trading route that ran through the state. The two main connecting towns were Black Foot and Tender Foot. Williams was running away from Tender Foot, and had no intention of going to Black Foot. Bad things happened at Black Foot. The local Sheriff there had been playing nursemaid to a group of Confederate soldiers still fighting the war a few months ago. No sir, there was no way that Sal Williams would be riding into that town.

As the dark night slowly enveloped him, Williams settled himself down. Tomorrow he would be home - in the cradle of his hometown.

But it was not to be.

A few hours later Sal would be found dead by a passing wanderer, he had become an unintentional player in a strange game.

* * *

Bolton Daniels had just found a body just where he was told it would be. It was the body of a tall, lean cowpoke. He checked the pockets of the dead man and found nothing. He picked the gun out of the dead man's holster and tucked it in the large back sack he carried everywhere with him.

"Mighty nice of you to leave these things to me," he said in gentlemanly voice tipping his ragged hat. "I've been looking for one of these Colts." He spun the cylinder checking its mechanism. "Fine gun. It's a shame you don't have any money."

Daniels then started to rifle through the dead man's saddlebags and, low and behold, he found himself a small money pouch. Looking inside the pouch he saw a small, but valuable, collection of old coins. He helped himself to the coins, took the dead man's hat – tossing his away - saddled up the dead man's horse and picked the blanket off the dead man's body.

He then removed his benefactor's boots, tunic and socks. Daniels looked around once more for any more items of value, and found none. He climbed onto his bequeathed horse and rode further down the trail.

Daniels was a wanderer, a vagabond and a scoundrel. He liked travelling around this great big country, and liked the things he found - or stole, even better. He even liked the women he sometimes visited in the brothels with other people's money. God had given him a fine, upstanding life bottom feeding off others. He would be heading back to Black Foot and he would gamble, drink and have a good time.

"Thank you, Mr Cow Poke," he said to himself.

It took about an hour for him to reach the busy settlement of Black Foot. He rode in, pulled up outside the saloon and stepped down from his horse.

"Mr Daniels," a voice said. "Welcome back to Black Foot."

"Well by-golly," Daniels said turning to face the voice. "What did I do wrong now, Mr. Crosby?"

"It's Sherriff Crosby and I see somehow you got yourself a horse," Billy replied. "And somehow you have money to spend at the saloon."

"Ain't nothin' illegal in either of those things," Daniels replied adamantly. "Ain't nothin' illegal on my person."

"Where did you get the horse?" Crosby asked patiently. "If you can't produce a bill of sale then I'm going to have to confiscate it."

"Now Mr – uh, Sherriff," the old wanderer said. "You can't be taking aim against me. I ain't done nothin' wrong."

"Like hell you haven't," Crosby said. "I want to search your back sack."

"You can't!" Daniels cried. "Ain't legal."

"See this badge? I'm the law around here," Crosby replied. "Want to change the law? Run for Congress."

Daniels lifted his back sack down from the back of the horse and placed it on the ground. He watched as Crosby bent down to go through his belongings.

Seeing his back sack being rummaged through, he couldn't stop himself. Daniels pulled his revolver out of his pocket and aimed it at Crosby.

It took a moment for Crosby to notice, and when he did he didn't flinch. He just shook his head in disgust and looked up at the old wanderer.

"Ain't a good idea," Crosby said slowly. "Ain't good at all."

"It's all I've got," Daniels said. "I can't let you take those things in there."

"I wasn't going to take anything that belonged to you," Crosby said. "I was just looking to see if you had anything belonging to people who don't happen to be called Bolton Daniels."

The old man let the revolver slip and Crosby made his move. He leapt forward, grabbed the gun and pointed it down toward the ground.

The old man looked startled and lost his grip and the gun fell to the ground forcing the old man to stumble backwards.

"You're under arrest," Crosby growled. "If I find anything in that back sack that doesn't belong to you, you're going away for a long time."

Daniels said nothing. He stood up straight and found himself walking towards the jail.

CHAPTER TWO

The days passed slowly as Daniels languished in jail. The Sheriff had nothing to keep him in jail for but kept him there anyway. Daniels could feel himself slowly rotting away. He was fed twice a day, but the food wasn't worth a damn. He longed for a juicy steak, or perhaps a few pieces of fruit. The rotgut he was given to eat didn't even satisfy his worms, and he had plenty of worms.

"Sheriff," he cried out. "When can I get out of this place?"

"As soon as you can tell me where the horse came from," Crosby hallowed back from the office. "Are you ready to tell me where you got it?"

"Won it," Daniels said loudly. "Won it in a game."

"A game of what?"

"Poker," Daniels replied glibly. "I won it from a man down in Tenderfoot."

"Liar," the Sheriff said. "Ain't no gambling houses in Tenderfoot. Only a fool would state that there is."

"Sure there is," Daniels retorted. "You just gotta know where to find them."

"Where then?" the Crosby asked walking into the cell block. "Where did you manage to get a game of poker in Tenderfoot?"

Daniels couldn't think of an answer fast enough. His old brain was failing him. It did that more often now, than it had before.

"See?" Crosby said. "You should think about your answer before you come griping to me about being stuck in jail. Are you going to tell me where you found that horse?"

Daniels sighed, "On a body," he sighed.

"On a body?" Crosby laughed. "You found a horse lying on a body?"

"No," Daniels retorted. "There was a dead man on that trail. Lying in the side of the road it was. I saw a perfectly good horse and..."

"And hat, and socks, and a gun..."

"Well, yes," Daniels said. "But it was all done legal like."

"And I guess you left that body out there to rot?"

"Well," Daniels said. "My body won't let me dig no holes for dead men. I'm an old man."

"Well get yourself ready," Crosby said. "We're going to go find that mystical body of yours and bury it all good and proper. You'll be digging the hole and I'll be resting myself on the back of my legally owned horse and watch."

"How am I going to get there?" Daniels asked.

"Walking. The way God intended men to travel."

"Well that just ain't fair," Daniels complained.

"Walk it, or stay here. Your choice."

* * *

The two men set out to where Daniels said the boy could be found. Daniels walked along in front of the Sheriff as they travelled through the Tumbleweed Pass.

A few years ago the previous Sheriff had been held hostage down there by a madman called Lucius. Billy's father, the richest man in town, had saved him and he'd slowly changed from a wild teenager, into a respectable man. His father had moved to San Francisco, and Billy had taken the post of Sheriff.

"Just a little farther along," Daniels grumbled. "Keeps a man's legs hurtin' when he has to walk this trail without a horse."

"You did it just fine before you stole that horse," Crosby said. "Keep walking."

"But my feet hurt," Daniels whined. "Can't I just get up there behind you on your horse?"

"Not a chance," the Sheriff replied. "Keep walking."

The little old man walked slowly along the path of the Tumbleweed Trail until he reached a turn - and turned left. The Sheriff followed him dutifully. The two men travelled for some time until the old man stopped, tumbled forward and fell on his face. Crosby jumped down from his horse and walked cautiously towards the old man.

"Get up ya' old cuss," Crosby said. "Still got a-ways to go. Ain't no swimming hole here so no use lying down on your front."

"Can't do it," the old man said weakly. "I just can't go any further."

Crosby kicked the old man and told him to get up again but Daniels just lay on the ground flat out. He turned slowly, panting and looked up at the young man.

"See that hollow over there," he said. "See it?"

Crosby looked over at the tree stump. He could see the top of it jutting out from the brush.

"I put some of my loot in that there stump," the old man said. "It's what you came here for, right?"

Crosby looked down at the old man. It smelt like a trap.

"Why don't you go fish it out," the Sheriff said.

"Ain't doing nothing of the kind," the old man stuttered. "If you want that there treasure- you go get it."

Crosby looked over at the large root. It was big enough to have plenty of wildlife living in it. He knew the chances - but if he was careful he could find whatever was in there, without being eaten alive. He walked over, knelt down and gently pushed his hand into the dark hole. He could feel nothing. His hand touched the bottom and then something bit into the fleshy part of his hand.

"It got you didn't it," the old man said climbing back to his feet. "It got you good. I knew it would—It always gets lawmen good."

The Sheriff watched as the old man smiled. Something that felt cold like a snake bit him. He pulled his hand back but the jaws of the snake held on tightly. He struggled with it until he passed out. The snake still gripped onto his hand like a dog holding a favorite stick.

"Got you good," the old man cackled. "You're deader than the man who owned that horse I stole."

Crosby lay still as the old man methodically went through his pockets. In a seemingly endless second wind he managed to find all the valuables, retrieve the Sheriff's gun and walked over to his horse.

"I'll see you in hell," Daniels said as he pointed the Sheriff's horse in the right direction and rode north. "I'm sure you'll get there before I do."

* * *

Crosby woke up inside a shack. There was no other way to describe it. He lay in a small bed staring up at the dark brown wood ceiling of the building - he had no recollection of what had befallen him. As he lay trying to work out how he found himself in such a place, he saw her. She was a stunning young woman with flowing red hair and as striking as a burning sunset.

"Who are you?" he said as she walked over to him.

"Doesn't matter - just eat." She placed a bowl of soup on the small table next to his pillow. He could smell the delicious soup, but he struggled to move.

"Still under the influence of that poison?" she asked.

He nodded. She sat down on the bed and picked up the small wooden bowl. Slowly she dipped the spoon into the soup and started feeding him. She said nothing more.

CHAPTER THREE

Daniels rode into Black Foot with an eye towards seeing a woman. He had plenty of money, plenty of time and, to his knowledge, nobody knew that he had killed the Sheriff. He was no longer a wanted man, or an escaped prisoner. He was just another old codger coming into a town filled with old codgers.

It wasn't the first time he had done such a thing. During the war he had killed many men, young, old, rich, poor, officers and common soldiers. This wasn't any different than the other killings he had been involved in. It just didn't feel finished.

He continued riding until he reached the house of ill repute and jumped down from the Sheriff's horse, tied her up and walked inside. He was met by the friendly smell of perfume. The first woman he would be dealing with would be Madame French.

"What'll you be having?" Madame French asked. "I remember you from last time," she added. "I don't want none of your tricks in here again—you ruined them two girls we imported from the continent."

Daniels smiled. The heavens were about to open. Those girls had sure spelled fun.

"Well?" she said. "Got a tongue?"

"I do," he replied. "How many of the girls can I have?"

Madam French clapped her hands and four beautiful girls came out from a side door. Daniels watched as the four prostitutes lined up. He pulled the money pouch from his pocket and ponied up.

"I will take all four," Daniels said gleefully.

"I thought that you would," the madam replied.

The tallest woman was the oldest. Her name was Gwen. The shortest girl was the second oldest. She was the curviest with beautiful blue eyes. Her name was Evie. Bolton thought the two youngest girls were the prettiest. Maybe they were sisters. Millie and Jenny were thin and both had deep, dark amazing brown eyes. The four escorted their John to a large bedroom with a large bed. There was also a nice, large comfortable chair in the room.

Daniels ordered Gwen and Evie to take off their clothes, jump into bed and make love to each other. This did not go over well with the two women. They gave Bolton a look of belligerence that infuriated the old man.

"Off with the clothes, now" Daniels growled as he pulled of his thick leather belt. "You will do as I say. I am the paying customer."

The women quickly disrobed.

"Both of you put the palm of your hands on the end of the bed and face the headboard", Daniels commanded. "Now stick your bare bottoms out towards me so I can have a little talk to them."

Daniels came in behind Gwen and within ten seconds he administered six hard, solid swats to her now inflamed backside with his doubled over belt. She fell forward with her elbows on the bed and started to cry. In an instant, he was behind Evie. Bolton thrashed Evie even harder than Gwen. However, Evie refused to cry. She helped Gwen onto the bed with her and fulfilled the perverted old man's command.

Daniels then preceded to drop his pants. He sat in the big chair and motioned the two young girls to kneel between his legs.

"This may be a tough job so it is fine if you alternate," Bolton said thinking he was being nice to the younger girls. "As for me, I am going to sit back and enjoy both shows."
`

Within fifteen minutes the old man was drained and happy. The women couldn't wait for him to leave. They collectively agreed he was their most despicable customer ever.

"Please Madam French," the four chimed at the same time, "never let him back in here again!"

Daniels turned away and walked over to the stagecoach depot. Black Foot was bustling with people and he had to wait for a few moments while the clerk took care of the couple booking tickets in front of him.

Finally it was his turn. "I want to book a ticket to Nevada," Daniels declared.

"Ain't but one coach going to Nevada," the clerk replied. "It'll be three dollars. You got three dollars?"

Daniels pulled the stolen pouch from his pocket and picked the coins from inside. He then slid them across to the clerk, who greedily took them and handed over a ticket.

"Coach is leaving on Sunday," the clerk said."

"Sunday?" Daniels replied. "I want to leave earlier than that."

"Coach will leave on Sunday," the clerk said again, pulling a blind down across the serving window.

Daniels stood for a few moments looking at his ticket. It wasn't perfect - but he could wait two days. The sheriff, after all, was dead.

Eventually Daniels turned and walked towards the barbers store. He intended to get his haircut then buy some new clothes for his new life in Nevada. Entering the barbers store he was immediately hit by the smell of tobacco.

"Cut?" the barber asked, a cigarette hanging from his bottom lip.

Daniels nodded and sat down in the chair.

The barber waivered for a few moments while he tried to work out what to do with the great mass of wadded hair sitting atop the old man's head. He then started to comb and shape. Soon the old man started to resemble a human being.

"Looks like it's been some time since you had a cut," the barber said.

"Yes," Daniels replied. "Bout twenty years."

The barber chuckled and continued working on the old man. Twenty minutes later he was finished. He held up a small handheld mirror in front of Daniels.

"I look pretty good," Daniels smiled.

"Better than you did when you came in," the barber replied. "Better than you've looked for twenty years, I'd say."

Daniels nodded and paid the man. Then he wandered over to the small clothing store on the other side of the street next to the Stage Depot. He walked in and bought two new suits, a pair of boots and a brand new hat. He then visited the gun store and bought a brand new belt and holster.

He looked at himself in the shop's looking glass and beamed. He was ready for his trip.

CHAPTER FOUR

"What happened?" Crosby said as he propped himself up in bed.

"I found you on the trail," the girl explained. "You were stupid enough to put your hand inside an old root and get bitten by one of the snakes that crawl at night."

"Shouldn't I be dead?" he asked. "Or am I dead?" He could be gazing at a heavenly creature. "Are you an angel?"

"No. You're not dead - and I sucked the poison from your wound. You could say that I'm your angel—but I sure don't feel like one—caring for you has taken up a good portion of my week."

"Daniels," the Sheriff said suddenly trying to sit up. "I'm coming for you," he said.

"You must be hallucinating," the girl replied. "I've had to do it a few times and sometimes the bite makes you see things."

"No," Crosby explained. "Daniels is a man—a dangerous man at that."

"Is he here in this room with us?" the girl said with a smile. "Maybe the poison went to your brain. I don't see any dangerous men in here."

"No I'm the Sheriff of Black Foot and I was with a man called Daniels. He tricked me into saying he had hidden some of his stolen loot inside that trunk."

"That trunk had nothing in it except a snake that got you," the girl said, pushing a lock of hair from in front of her hazel eyes. "You should'a know better than to put your hand inside strange trunks on the trails."

"I need to get back to Black Foot," he said, trying to lift himself out of bed. But his arms were shaky. He couldn't hold himself up. Soon his arms gave way and he fell back into bed.

"You're in no condition to move," the girl said. "Try resting."

"What's your name?" Crosby asked. "I'm Billy."

"Billy," she said with a smile. "My name is Charlene, but my friends call me Carrie."

"Well Carrie. I need you to help me."

"Do what?" she asked.

"I need you to get me back to Black Foot. I'm the Sheriff of the town and I need to report an escaped felon. His name is Bolton Daniels and he's armed, dangerous and I'm a fool for ever believing he would tell me a truthful thing."

"You can't move for the next few days, it could be dangerous."

"I'm paid for danger," he exclaimed. "Get me out of this damn bed."

Carrie felt like refusing him, but didn't. She helped Crosby out of bed and into a chair that stood on the other side of the table.

"Can I have my boots?"

"You didn't have any when I found you," she explained. "All you had is what you're wearing right now."

"Daniels must have taken them," Crosby said angrily. "Okay do you have a horse?"

"No. Don't have nothing but a mule."

"The mule will do."

Carrie helped the weak Crosby outside and sat him down on a rock while she readied the mule for travelling. Soon the two of them were riding slowly down the trail.

Her home seemed to be set back off the side of the trail behind the ridges. This would be a longer journey, but once they got to Black Foot he could wire the Rangers and have them begin their search for Daniels. Then he could rest for a few hours and head out to look for him.

"You are in no state to be travelling," Carrie chided, as the two of them rode along. "You should have stayed in bed."

"I can't let him get away," Crosby said. "I picked him up a few days ago with a new horse in town," he explained. "I kept him in the cells for a few days and he finally admitted that he'd stolen it from a dead man he had found on this trail. We were heading back down the trail to try and find the body. For my money, I think he killed that man."

"You think?" Carrie asked. "Where was this dead man?"

"Bout a mile from where you found me. Why?"

"No reason," Carrie replied flatly. "But I haven't seen any dead men on the trail and I walk quite often. I tend to go into Black Foot for my supplies."

"You may know Daniels," the sheriff said. "He's a wanderer who makes it his business to be involved in anything he can get his beak into."

Carrie laughed but said nothing.

"Well?" Crosby pressed. "Have you seen him?"

"I don't think so," she said after a moment of thought. "May have seen him, but I don't really get involved in other's business."

"I understand."

The two of them rode in silence the rest of the way. The journey seemed longer when taken on a mule. As the ornery creature crept along slowly, Crosby could feel himself falling asleep, but he fought it off.

Another bend in the trail and the two of them could see Black Foot in the distance.

Michael Haden

CHAPTER FIVE

"There's a card game going in town," a rotund man with handlebar moustache told Daniels drinking at saloon. "Do you want in? It looks likely to be a good one"

Daniels thought for a few moments. A card game could give him the collateral to start a new life in Nevada. It could also get him thrown in jail.

"How many people attending?" Daniels asked. "I ain't doing it if half the town is going to be there."

"Just a few of us," the man said stroking his moustache. "It won't be much of a public attraction."

"That's what you said last time, Porter," Daniels cursed. "I had to crawl through the damn window and run deep into the trail," he seethed. "Even then they nearly got me."

"Won't be like that this time," Porter promised. "By the way. You sure do look like you have been doing well."

"I ain't been doing too bad," Daniels said. "Where the game?"

"It's down at the backend of town behind the general store. Be good to see you there, Bolton."

"Well I may consider it," Daniels replied. "No promises."

The idea of moving to Nevada seemed like a great idea to Daniels, to begin with. But now the reality was starting to kick in. How would he support himself in this Daniels new place? He was being accustomed to all the nice things in life. These clothes, the haircut. Life was starting to get complicated for him at the age of sixty.

But sooner, rather than later, there would be questions about the missing Sheriff, and there may have been someone who saw him leave Black Foot with Daniels.

Still, that wouldn't prove anything, but it would be enough for someone to start asking embarrassing questions. The questions would lead to a cell and the cell would lead to the hanging tree. Daniels, knew as soon as he remembered the cell he had just escaped, that he would be attending that illegal card game.

* * *

Crosby eventually arrived at Black Foot and, with Carrie's help, climbed down from the mule. His whole body ached and as she helped him into his office the townsfolk started to gather outside to find out what had happened to him.

"Did the injuns get him?" one man asked.

"Nah," another said. "It was more of them Confederates."

Once inside his office, Crosby eased into the plush chair behind his desk and leaned back.

"Let them in," he said. "I don't want rumours getting around town that the Sheriff is dying or something."

"Let them wait," Carrie said coldly. "You need to rest,"

"To hell with rest," Crosby cried, leaning forward.

"Sure," Carrie said. "And what happens if your body fails when you are in the middle of a gunfight? What happens if you have a relapse?"

"Ain't nothing wrong with me," Crosby retorted.

"Rest," Carrie soothed. "Just rest."

"Get me my boots, get me my spare gun and I'll be fine. Just do what I ask woman."

"You do it yourself," she shot back. "I'm going back home."

"Then go," he screamed as she walked out of his office. He felt instant remorse, but managed to pull himself together enough to get to his feet and collect his spare boots from the cabinet that lined the back wall of his office. He also grabbed his spare colt, and redeemed a bottle of whisky he had been saving for a special occasion.

All done, he sat back down in his chair, took a long swig of whisky and pulled his boots on. He was going to go after Daniels, and dead or alive he would be returning to Black Foot. As he struggled with the laces of his boots, a knock came to the door of his office.

"Come in," the sheriff called out.

"Sheriff," a hefty black man wearing a small cap said. "What happened to you? The townsfolk are saying that those Confederates have returned. Is that true?"

"No. This is the result of one old wandering scoundrel."

"Daniels?" the man asked.

"Cletus," Crosby asked, "how would a nice guy like you know about Bolton Daniels."

"Simple," Cletus replied with a smile. "He owned me for a while."

Cletus was a free black man who had been free as long as the sheriff had known him. The idea of Cletus Brown being a slave was as alien to Billy Crosby as the President being a crook.

"When did he own you?" the sheriff asked.

"Back before the war. I saw him with you the other day - he's a mighty mean man, Sherriff. Sneaky, very sneaky when he wants to be."

"I found *that* out," Crosby replied, rubbing his hand.

"He hasn't always been old and doddering," Cletus explained. "When he was young he tried every job, but gambler worked best for him. He ended up owning me after a match with my owner up until then, if you know what I mean."

"I think I understand," Crosby said with a grin. "So what happened?"

Cletus shrugged, "War came and he couldn't own me no more."

"How did you end up here?" Crosby asked the old black man. "Didn't you want to be truly free and go a long way away from Daniels?"

"No sir," Cletus replied grinning. "I always liked it around here, it felt like home, and besides I was married to Betsy."

"I've known about Bolton Daniels most of my life," Crosby stated. "My father always said that he chickened out of fighting that Confederate attack off — but his wife at the time was happy to help them out."

"That sounds about right," Cletus said. "I fought in that fight and it was a mighty good one," he said proudly. "I never enjoyed a fight more than that."

"My father said it was pretty close. I always thought Daniels was a wandering coward. I never realized that he had been so involved in things around here."

"He's always been involved in the bad things," Cletus replied. "He's never done a good thing in his life."

"Do you think he's capable of killing a man?"

"Oh yes," Cletus replied. "He can do that with no problems. I saw him kill several guys. He likes to knife them in the back when they ain't lookin'."

"I think he killed a man on the trail," Crosby stated.. "I think he killed him in cold blood and I think he stole everything that man owned."

"Sounds about right to me," Cletus agreed. His expressive brow bent in sorrow. "I just wish he'd died years ago. I wish someone had just killed that miserable son of a bitch."

"What happened to his wife?" the sheriff asked.

"She died. She had a hard life. He had a daughter too. I don't know what happened to her."

"I didn't know he had a daughter," Crosby said in surprise.

"Sure. He had a daughter with his wife. They left together after Daniels tried to kill her."

"He tried to kill his daughter?" Crosby asked astounded.

"Yes, sir," Cletus said. "Tried to kill her with a knife when she was real young," Cletus explained. "That's why his wife finally left him."

"Why?" Crosby asked.

"Drink," Cletus replied.

"I wish someone had killed him too," Crosby said amazed by this new history about a man he always knew as an old wanderer. "Tell me. Did you see a girl out there? The girl I came to town with?"

"Yes," Cletus said. "I did, she looked like she was getting ready to leave."

"I need to go apologize," Crosby said. "She helped me out and I snapped."

"Sounds like love to me, boss," Cletus said as his grin returned. "Want me to go get her?"

"If you wouldn't mind. I would be most grateful."

Cletus left the office and came back a few moments later with Carrie in tow. "I just want to say something before I leave," Cletus said. "I know you want to be private together. But I want to ride with you when you go after Daniels."

"You know I'm going after him?" Crosby said.

"I figured as much," Cletus said. "It makes sense that a good man like you would want to kill a bad man like him."

"I'll be riding out today. I would appreciate you coming along."

Cletus left and Crosby could hear him telling the townsfolk outside the office about the sheriff and his mission. Several of them chimed in agreement. No one was surprised to hear that Daniels was under investigation for murder.

"So why did you want to see me again?" Carrie asked. "I need to go back home."

"Look I appreciate the help you gave me. I truly do and I would like it if you would stay in town."

"Why? You think I want to be seen with a beat up old Sheriff?"

"Maybe. Maybe I just want to thank you for helping me out."

"All men only want one thing," Carrie snorted. "All men just want what women can give them. My daddy used to say that man was only interested in one thing - and that one thing was truly evil."

"Your daddy was wrong," Crosby countered. "Not all men are like that."

"Just most of them," Carrie shot back. "I have no interest in being your concubine, Sheriff."

"Then how about being my friend?" Crosby suggested.

"Well," Carrie said softly. "We can see about that."

"I need a few hours sleep…" the sheriff started to explain.

"You need more than a few hours," Carrie shot back incensed. "You don't have to go after Daniels, you don't have to do any of this. You can go to bed and know that you did as much as any man in this town to try and find out who killed that man."

"No," Crosby retorted. "My father took on an army to save me from murderers. I won't stand back unless I have done that same thing for someone else. It wouldn't be right, and it's not me."

"Then you're a fool," Carrie screamed. "But," she said. "If you have to go, I will go with you."

"I'd appreciate that. I'd like it if you would nurse me through this challenge."

"I'll do my best."

CHAPTER SIX

"Mighty nice of you to show up for the game," a tall thin, leathery looking, pimple faced man said holding his hand out to shake hands. "My name is Sam and I'll be your host tonight."

Daniels shook the man's outstretched hand and grunted something unintelligible. He walked over and took a seat, taking great care to not crease his brand new trousers. He then watched as other players filed into the room.

As soon as Sam was satisfied the last player had arrived he moved over to the table and took a seat at its end.

"Welcome to the game," he said. "Since they made gambling illegal in this town we make do with private meets like this. Now there is a chance that the sheriff will show up but until then, let's play."

The cards were dealt and Daniels played well. His pot started to build and his opponents started to lose and lose big. He could see the strain on the face of the man who sat across from him. The painted smile he had worn at the beginning of the game had soured by the middle.

Daniels felt sorry for him, but took his money anyway. Lost in the game at hand the knock on the door was almost missed by the players. Nobody missed the second knock when the Marshall of territory came hurtling through the door.

"Hands up," he shouted. "You're all under arrest."

Daniels shrunk back in his seat and watched as the Marshall circled around the game. He thought quickly. He needed a diversion.

"Now look Marshall Houston," Sam pleaded. "This is a private game and we aren't gambling."

"Then what's with the money," Houston said. "Looks like gambling to me."

"No," Sam objected. "We've been raising money for the orphan's home on the edge of town. You know the one run by old lady Wilkins."

"Then you won't mind if we take this money and bring it down to the orphan's home, then will you?" Houston asked with a wry smile.

"Well," Sam said with a stutter. "Maybe not all of it," he explained. "See some of it was just the men counting out how much they had."

"No," the Marshall said. "I think the money on this table may save the necks of the men sitting at it."

Daniels fingered the gun in its holster hanging from his waist. He was ready to use it. But he didn't have to. Sam was going to be the one to take chances. Daniels watched as Sam's hand slid slowly beneath the table. He waited, and waited, and waited.

"Marshall," Sam said. "Can we talk privately, like?"

Houston nodded under his ten-gallon hat and Sam rose quickly, too quickly to be countered. He fired three shots into the Marshall's body and the surprised lawman fell backwards.

All the other men at the table sat rigidly in their chairs.

"What the hell have you done?" one of them asked. "You killed Marshall Houston!"

"He was old and dumb anyways," Sam sneered. "But we have to get rid of the body. Help me drag it out onto the street, Janus."

The men stood up and watched as Sam and Janus dragged the Marshall's lifeless body out of the building.

Daniels saw his chance and started collecting the pot. He also collected the last few bills and coins from the man who had been sitting to his left, and for good measure took the bills from the man who had been sitting to his right. He left the man a few paltry coins.

Then Daniels stood and slowly made his way to the back entrance of the establishment. He was gone before the other men noticed and the most beautiful thing was that none of those men could ever come after him for taking that money. Not without implicating themselves in the murder of the Marshall.

What worried Daniels though, was that he could become the suspect in that killing too. He couldn't afford to wait around for the stage now. He would have to head back to the only place he could go. He would have to visit his daughter.

* * *

The few hours of sleep had actually turned into a full night of sleep. It was Saturday morning before the world saw Sheriff Crosby again. He lay in the bunk he kept in the back room of his office and slept the sleep of the dead. When he finally found himself awake again he felt groggy. It took a coffee and a smile from the beautiful Carrie to bring him back to the world.

"How was your sleep?" she asked. "I didn't want to wake you as you looked so peaceful."

"Well," he said. "I've slept worse than that."

"That black fella has been in a few times to see you," Carrie said. "He seemed mighty upset that you weren't ready to go on the trail."

"Cletus is a good man," Crosby said, pouring himself another coffee. "You see I found out yesterday that he once belonged to Daniels. I also found out that the old man had a daughter."

"You did?" Carrie said surprised. "I didn't think he sounded like the kind of man who would have a daughter."

"No. And apparently he tried to kill her. Can you imagine such a thing?"

"I can't," Carrie replied. "Do you want bacon and eggs? Or would you prefer beans?"

"I'd prefer bacon, eggs and some beans, please. I would also like to know how long you've been living on the Tumbleweed Trail."

"Ever since I was a kid," she replied getting ready to make breakfast. "It was all I ever knew. Ma and I would wait for daddy to come home each night with something to eat, and perhaps some news from Tender Foot."

"Didn't you ever want to get married before?" Crosby asked taking another sip of the boiling hot coffee. "Haven't you ever wanted that?"

"Not until recently," Carrie said with a smile. "I never knew a man, 'cept my father. Until I met you," she said coyly.

"Well, you know, there are many men in this world who would love to have a beautiful girl like you to be their wife," Crosby said. The smell of the bacon cooking in the griddle and the sight of a girl as attractive as Carrie working hard in the kitchen was something that would make many men very happy.

"Maybe," Carrie said. "How do you like your eggs?"

* * *

A full hour later, filled with coffee and a good meal, Crosby walked out of his office and found Cletus sitting across the street at the stable. He was waiting for him.

"Sheriff!" he called. "You ready to go out yet and get Daniels?"

"Almost," Crosby called back. "I just need to go see someone."

Crosby, still aching from the remnants of the poison, walked down the right hand side of the main street. He needed to speak with someone urgently. That man was called Bridger. His full title was Captain Bridger.

Crosby stopped at a small alleyway that led to the back of a gun store. He walked down and knocked on a small door to his left.

"Bridger," he called out. "Are you awake yet? Bridger?"

"Who is it?" a sleepy voice called out. "This is too early to be waking up old soldiers."

The door opened and Crosby smiled as he saw an older, but still youthful looking man - Captain Bridger. The savior of the town of Black Foot.

"Now what can I do to help you, Billy?" he asked looking puzzled. "And no I ain't going to lead another damn fool cavalry charge down the middle of high street," he said with a laugh.

"I don't need that from you today," Crosby said. "But tell me do you know a man called Bolton Daniels?"

"Heard of him," Bridger said. "He used to come down to the camp we had on the trail and sell the Colonel pelts, guns and the like. I always thought they looked stolen."

"Ever have any dealings with him? The reason I ask is that I had him held up in town a few days ago as I thought he'd stolen a horse and some other items. He admitted to finding them out on the trail. I took him out there and he somehow coerced me to put my hand down a stump. I got bit by some snake and now I'm trying to find out more about him. Cletus Brown came by yesterday and told me he had a daughter."

"That's right," Bridger said. "He did have a daughter. He had a wife. You know his wife fought in that battle we had in town."

"That's what Cletus said. Ever meet the daughter?"

"Can't say I have, but I heard he tried to kill her. Your father would know more about it. He was the man who stopped him from doing it."

"He never told me."

"No it happened while you were at military school," Bridger explained. "It was several years ago now. Ancient history."

"Ever know what happened to the wife and daughter?"

"Sure," Bridger said. "They left town. You know the best thing you could do would be to wire you father over in San Francisco and find out more. He would know best."

"I will. I'll do that. Thanks Captain." Crosby threw him a half-assed salute.

"Get out of here ya' bum," Bridger smiled. "And nice to see you back around town again. You should pop in when ma is awake and say howdy."

"I will. Maybe when I get back from catching Daniels."

"Good luck. You'll need it." Bridger said with a smile as he closed the door.

Crosby made his way back to the main street and walked down to the wire office. He stood at the small queue that had collected at the office window and waited his turn.

The day was turning out to be a good one. A strong blue sky, with few clouds. The lady in front was taking her time sending a wire to her son in Canada, but as soon as she finished her message she left.

"I want to send a wire to my father," Crosby told Joe, the operator.

"Sure thing," Joe said. "Let me get my pencil sharpened."

The two of them made small talk as the old man sharpened his pencil. "Now what do you want to say to your pa?" Joe asked.

"Need to know everything you know about Bolton Daniels. Regards, Billy."

"Is that it?" Joe said surprised. "Nothing more than that?"

"Well, Not really."

"Well how about that?" Joe remarked. "A man who can send a telegram without reciting the dictionary."

"How about that?" Crosby chided. "See you later Joe."

"See you, Billy," Joe replied with a smile. "And if you're looking for Daniels - don't underestimate him. He's a Daniels bird by nature, as well as by name."

"That," Crosby said. "is what I'm starting to learn."

CHAPTER SEVEN

"The lure of the tumbleweed," Daniels sang as he rode into the passage that led from Black Foot. "The lure is that you never get out, if you get in, and when you get in you can never get out..." He laughed at the words.

It was a mighty fine day for visiting his daughter. He knew that. He also knew that she would be fiercely against his visit until he charmed her a little. After all, he had told her already that he hadn't meant to try to kill her. He was just under the influence of a little bit of bad moonshine at the time. It stood to common sense that a man who drank bad moonshine would, perhaps, do bad things. Still he would smooth her over and she would cook for him, and allow him to hold up for a few days until things settled down in Black Foot. Then he could go down, book another ticket for the stagecoach and be on his way to Nevada.

Perhaps, he thought, she would like to come with him?

He took the left hand turn that led away from the trail and went up the narrow path that led to the top of the ridge. He then stepped down from his horse and led her the rest of the way. The shack that his daughter called home was nestled at the back of the ridge.

"Are you around?" he called as he tied his horse to one of the closest trees to the shack. "Hello?"

There was no answer. He walked towards the shack, opened the door and made himself at home. It was a tidy little living space - very much like the living space of a spinster. He helped himself to some fruit on the table and opened up his pouch of tobacco, rolled a cigarette – and waited.

He knew she would be home sooner, rather than later.

* * *

Crosby returned to his office and Carrie was waiting for him. "You still want to come with me?" he asked.

She nodded.

"OK. Let's find Cletus. Should be waiting in the saloon."

The two walked over to the saloon and found Cletus waiting at the bar nursing a beer. "Ready to go get Daniels?" Crosby asked.

"You bet, Sheriff," Cletus replied.

"Let's mount up," Crosby said.

CHAPTER EIGHT

A few hours on the Tumbleweed Trail passed when Carrie asked, "Can we stop by my cabin? I need to pick up a few things. Don't know how long we'll be out looking."

Crosby agreed and they took the left hand turn that led away from the trail and went up the narrow path that led to the top of the ridge. The shack that she called home was nestled at the back of the ridge.

Seeing the shack, Crosby said, "We'll walk the horses the rest of the way."

When they arrived at the cabin, they noticed a lone horse tethered to the fence.

"You expecting company," Crosby asked Carrie.

She shook her red locks. "I'll find out. Wait here"

She takes off for the cabin while Cletus and Crosby watch cautiously.

Carrie entered the cabin when Cletus said, "I think we should follow her."

"You're probably right," Crosby replied.

* * *

When Carrie opened the door to her cabin, she gasped.

"What? No welcome for your father?" Daniels chuckled. "No kiss?"

45

Carrie gave him a look of disgust and went towards the bedroom just as Crosby and Cletus entered the shack.

Immediately, Daniels pulled his gun on the two. "Take it easy Sheriff. Just visiting my daughter one last time before I catch the stage and head out of the territory."

"Then why the gun?" asked Crosby.

"Just to make sure our conversation stays friendly. Besides, she's been a good help to an old man. Haven't you Carrie?"

The young woman's face turned white. Crosby's face was a question mark. "What are talking about?"

"Should I tell them Carrie – or you."

"Don't believe him, Billy," she pleaded.

"Oh come one. Tell the Sheriff how you were so helpful to your old man," Daniels grinned.

Carrie said nothing. She just stood there frozen in fear.

"Ok. I'll tell him." Daniels kept waving his pistol at Crosby and Cletus then his tone turned ominous. "This sweet young lady is a murderer."

"Don't believe him!" Carrie shouted.

"Shut up!" he barked at Carrie. Then turned back to Crosby. "She's been killing pilgrims on the Tumbleweed Trail and leaving their bodies for me to rob." He hideously grinned. "Like that cowpoke you were so bent on burying."

"Carrie," asked Crosby. "Why?"

Carrie started to cry and between her tears she explained how her father tried to kill her as a child and made her kill those travellers.

"But why did you agree to do it?" asked Crosby stunned.

"Because if I didn't he would beat me like he used to beat my mom. My mother died of a broken heart. All the abuse from my father killed her. "We tried to run from him but he would hunt us down."

Daniels roared with laughter. "A father and his dear daughter. Blood *is* thicker than water, huh Crosby. Thank you dear." He tipped his hat and pointed his gun right at Crosby. "Now take his gun, my dear, and do your father another favor. *Kill him*," he scowled.

Carrie walked over and pulled Crosby's gun from his holster and pointed it at him.

"Good girl. Now *shoot* him!"

Shocking everyone, Carrie turns the gun on Daniels. "No! You...!"

But Daniels was quick and shot her before she could fire her gun. She collapsed on the floor clutching her chest – a red stain flowing from between her fingers.

But Crosby saw his chance and he rushed Daniels. Cletus joined him.

Crosby knocked Daniels into and over a small table and onto the floor while Cletus tried to wrestle Daniels's gun from his hand.

But Cletus only gets shot in the shoulder for his trouble and Daniels pushed Crosby off of him.

In a split second, Daniels took the opportunity to race out to his horse.

Crosby rushes over to Carrie and she coughs, "I should never have trusted him... even if he was my father."

Cletus, back on his feet, wounded but not dead, came over to Crosby and leaned over the seriously wounded girl. He hands Crosby his gun and looks at Crosby and shakes his head.

"Are you alright?" Crosby asked.

"I'll live," Cletus replied.

"I want you to stay with Carrie." Then Crosby gritted his teeth. "I'm going after Daniels."

Crosby ran out to his horse, jumps on it and chased after Daniels.

Michael Haden

CHAPTER NINE

Daniels had two options. He could try to ride out of the territory or he can try to make it to the stage. He decided to make a try with his horse.

As he rode onto the tail, he saw Crosby gaining on him. He knew Crosby wouldn't rest now until he was dead.

Daniels beat on his horse but Crosby was still gaining. He looked ahead and saw the stage rumbling along.

Six horses are better than one, he thought.

Daniels pressed his horse forward while firing back at Crosby.

The shots missed and Crosby fired back.

Daniels drew alongside the stagecoach under galloping hooves and grabbed the door of the coach. He pulled himself from his horse and hung from the side of the stage, his feet dragging, trying to get a foothold.

The door swung open and a woman screamed! Daniels saw two men and a woman inside the cab.

"What the hell are you doing?" demanded one of the men.

Daniels didn't miss a beat and fired blindly into the coach not caring who shot, then climbed up to the surprised driver.

The rotund driver reached for his shotgun under his feet but Daniels shoved his bulk off the stage under the racing coach then jumped into the driver's seat whipping the horses into frenzy as they ran.

Crosby rode up behind the stage, jumped onto its back, then climbed hand-over-hand to the top.

Daniels turned to see where Crosby was, saw him almost on top of him, fired his pistol and blew Crosby's hat off.

Crosby, in the open, lunged from the top of the coach under the stage and held on for dear life.

"Got 'em," Daniels laughed.

But Crosby slowly made his way under the coach to the front of the hitch and managed to unhook the horses.

The sudden release of the six-horse team made the coach run wild ending up tipping over on its side. It scoured along the trail spitting out pieces of wood and metal as it came apart under them.

The coach finally came to stop, on it's side - wheels spinning in the air.

All was quiet for a while when Crosby shook himself awake and focused on his dilemma. He was a bloody mess. His body was a mass of cuts and abrasions and when he tried to stand up, a burning pain shot through his right leg. He feared his leg was broken.

Daniels was on his feet and walking towards him – gun drawn. Crosby reached for his holster and pulled out his gun. With one shot he rid the world of Bolton Daniels.

Without delay he was back in the saddle speeding back to Carrie's cabin.

* * *

From that moment on nothing was as important to Billy Crosby as was Carrie's well-being. The ride back to her cabin seemed to take forever. When he finally got to his destination Cletus was addressing Carrie's wound.

"I think I got the bleeding stopped," Cletus informed Billy. "The combination of her wearing a thick corset, being well endowed and the bullet hitting square on the rib and not the easily penetrable cartilage in between the ribs, the bullet did not penetrate the heart or its vessels. I was able to pull out the bullet without too much loss of blood."

"She looks so pale and lifeless," Billy lamented. "Do you think she will be able to pull through?"

"It is hard to say," Cletus responded. "One thing is for sure. That old bastard Bolton was shooting to kill. How can a man do that to his own daughter?"

"I don't know," Billy said shaking his head. "Please take my badge back to Black Foot and please be its sheriff for a little while until I get back. I need to stay with Carrie until she gets better."

With Cletus gone, all Billy could do is pray and keep Carrie hydrated. Carrie was barely lucid but she enjoyed having Billy tell her stories he remembered from the Bible. He sat with her day and night holding her hand or rubbing her shoulders or feet.

Soon, Carrie was getting stronger and was even able to eat. Cletus had sent a doctor to the cabin with medicine to prevent infection from setting into the wound. The area she was shot was extremely green, inflamed and filled with puss.

"Take these antibiotics and I will check back with you in about a week," the doctor instructed. "I really don't like how the wound is healing."

As the doctor rode off, Carrie insisted she felt fine.

"Carrie, if you make it through this, I promise you the biggest wedding in Black Foot history. I want to show you off as mine to the entire town.'
"That is very sweet, Carrie responded. "Whether I make it through this or not, there is one thing I want to do with you."

Carrie and Billy embraced in a long, deep sensual kiss. Their clothes were quickly strewn on the floor and Billy did everything to position his weight away from Carrie's chest. Passionately, hard muscle and soft flesh became one as Carrie and Billy consummated their love for each other.

The next few days were pure bliss for Carrie and Billy. They even went for a long walk as Carrie became stronger. Tragically, Carrie's recovery took a turn for the worse. She was once again bed ridden.

"I've been afraid to ask you this question," Carrie said weakly. What ended up happening to my father?

"Justice was served," Billy answered. "His life had to be ended for the good of everyone. He will never be able to hurt you ever again."

Carrie wept. Bolton Daniels was her father and as much as she distained him she did have some love in her heart for him.

"Carrie, your wounds look worse than ever. I am going into town to get the doctor back here.

"Please don't leave me, Carrie begged. "The doctor said he will come back in a few days on his own and I will double down on the medicine he gave me until he gets back."

"If this is your wish I will honor it,' he said. With that said Carrie went to sleep. Billy held her hand the entire time.

Late that night a dark evil spirit entered the dwelling. He sucked the last breath from Carrie's lungs.

Billy Crosby broke down and cried profusely. As the phantom left Carrie's home he was heard to say: "You may have taken my life, but you can't have my daughter."

The End

Printed in Great Britain
by Amazon